MW00885768
This dragon book belongs to:
....

The Yoga Dragon
My Dragon Books - Volume 4
Written by Steve Herman

Published by DG Books Publishing, an imprint of Digital Golden Solutions LLC.

ISBN: 978-1948040136 (paperback)
ISBN: 978-1948040297 (hardcover)

www.MyDragonBooks.com

First Edition: February 2018
10 9 8 7 6 5 4 3 2 1

The Yoga Dragon
My Dragon Books - Volume 4
Steve Herman

Hello! Nice to meet you. My name is Drew. I have a well-trained dragon by the name of Diggory Doo.

You can teach your dragon tricks,
but one thing you must require –
You have to train your dragon not
to set your house on fire!

If you see an angry dragon
or one that’s feeling stressed,
Or a dragon acting cranky
‘cause he didn’t get his rest…

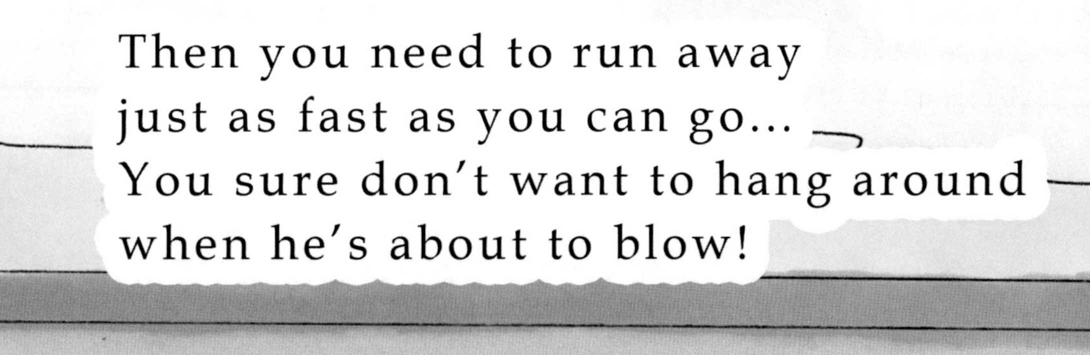
Then you need to run away
just as fast as you can go...
You sure don't want to hang around
when he's about to blow!

One time my dragon sniffed
as if he was about to cry...

Then he hung his scaly head
and exhaled a smoky sigh.

I patted his head, and then I said,
"Diggory Doo, what's wrong?"

"I'm tired and stressed,"
my dragon confessed,
"from working all day long."

“First I picked up all my toys,
and then I made my bed…”

"Swept the floor and so much more;
I'm worn out," Diggory said.

"Diggory Doo, this will not do,"
I said with much concern –

"**YOGA** will help you
deal with stress,
which I can help you learn."

"For instance, when you're working hard,
then you should pause a bit.
For even dragons need to rest,
so take a break and sit."

Diggory sat and crossed his legs
(I had to show him how)
He took a few deep breaths
and said, “I feel much better now!”

EASY POSE!

I said, "Even though our chores are essential things to do,
We must make time to play each day, for that's important, too."

z z Z Z

"Practice balance in your life;
I'm sure you won't regret it –
Here's a trick that you can do
to help you not forget it..."

"Since you're reaching for a better life,
reach high up in the air,
Then stand upon one foot awhile
and try to balance there."
TREE POSE!

One day when it was raining
and he had to play inside,

Diggory Doo was disappointed,
so he pouted and he cried.

CRESCENT MOON!

I said, "We must adjust when what
we want just cannot be,
So bend from side to side to
prove your flexibility!"

One time Diggory Doo was sick
and had to see the vet
He shook a bit and bit his lip;
his tummy was upset.

I reassured my dragon,
and I gave his head a pat –
"We all get scared at times,"
I said, "but there's a cure for that!"

"It's an easy exercise to do;
this is how it goes –
Just bend over at the waist,
then you reach down to
your toes"

"Stretch your back as you relax,
and hang there for a while;
Let the tension leave your body,
and you soon will find your smile."

"And even though you may think
it's a silly thing to do,
Here's a way to turn your back
on whatever troubles you..."
DOWNWARD-
FACING DOG!

"You place your hands down on the floor and stick out your behind,
And when troubles come to visit, don't pay them any mind!"

WARRIOR II
"Then stand and spread your arms to give the world a big embrace, For all the things you love in life which you cannot replace."

Don't let your problems get you down
but focus on what's good –
Learn Yoga, too, like Diggory Doo –
I really think you should!

Get your FREE Gift from Diggory Doo at
www.MyDragonBooks.com/gift

Read more about Drew and Diggory Doo!

Visit
www.MyDragonBooks.com
for more!

If you like this book, can you go to
Amazon and write about what you think?
It will help parents and other awesome kids
like you know what to expect from this book!
I'd love to read about your thought!
THANK YOU!